# Charlie
## & The Great Escape

Look out for other books in this series:

# Charlie
## & The Cat Flap

# Charlie
## & The Big Snow

www.hilarymckay.co.uk

# Charlie
## & The Great Escape

# Hilary McKay

## Illustrated by Sam Hearn

**M**SCHOLASTIC

First published in the UK in 2007 by Scholastic Children's Books
An imprint of Scholastic Ltd
Euston House, 24 Eversholt Street
London, NW1 1DB, UK
Registered office: Westfield Road, Southam, Warwickshire, CV47 0RA
SCHOLASTIC and associated logos are trademarks and or
registered trademarks of Scholastic Inc.

Text copyright © Hilary McKay, 2007
Illustrations © Sam Hearn, 2007
The right of Hilary McKay to be identified as the author of this work
and of Sam Hearn to be identified as the illustrator of this work has
been asserted by them.

10 digit ISBN 0 439 94429 5
13 digit ISBN 978 0439 94429 8

Typeset by Falcon
Printed in the UK by CPI Bookmarque, Croydon, CR0 4TD
Papers used by Scholastic Children's Books are
made from wood grown in sustainable forests.

7 9 10 8 6

www.scholastic.co.uk/zone

# ONE

## Going

Charlie had a very sad hard life. He had a terrible family who did not appreciate him.

Charlie was seven years old and he lived with his brother Max, who was eleven years old, and his father and mother, who were ancient.

"They like Max best," Charlie told his best friend Henry.

It was a sunny afternoon in the summer holidays. Charlie was spending it in Henry's garden, which was just down the road from his own. He was having a good grumble.

"They like Max *much* better than me! They laugh at *his* jokes. . ."

"Don't they laugh at yours?"

"No," said Charlie. "They say stuff like, 'Charlie, that is not the sort of thing anyone wants to hear about at the dinner table'. And they hate my mouth-organ playing. My dad shouts, 'Somewhere else, please Charlie!' the second I begin."

"My mum *asks* me to play my recorder," remarked Henry smugly.

"*My* mum," said Charlie, "groans when

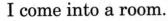

I come into a room. And says, 'Shoes off, Charlie, before you take another step!' And she goes on and on about interrupting people talking. How can I not interrupt when she talks all the time? I have to yell to make her take any notice of me."

"I've heard you," agreed Henry. "If your front door's open we can hear you right down the road."

"And the fuss she makes if I come home in the wrong clothes if I've accidentally put on someone else's after PE! Or about lost socks! My mum's got a thing about socks. Every time I come home without them she goes mad!"

"What does it matter about losing socks?" asked Henry in astonishment. "Everyone has socks! I have thousands!"

"I have three," said Charlie. "Borrow Max's."

"Oh ha ha ha," said Charlie bitterly. "As if that could ever happen! *None* of my family share *anything* with me."

"*I* share with you," said Henry. "At least you've got *me*."

"S'pose," said Charlie ungratefully.

"And when you're grown up you can run away from your terrible family!"

"I could run away now," said Charlie. "That would show them! Then they'd be sorry!"

"They might be *pleased*," remarked Henry. "Then what?"

Instead of answering that unsympathetic question, Charlie rugby-tackled Henry's knees. They fell together in a scuffling heap on top of Henry's mother's washing basket, which was full of clean wet washing waiting for a space on the line. Henry grabbed a T-shirt and washed Charlie's face with it. Charlie stuffed a pair of damp pants down Henry's neck. For the next few minutes they whacked each other with bunches of wet socks. After that Charlie got Henry flat on his back and very cleverly managed to force Henry's mother's nightdress over his head, proving he had won. Henry pulled it off and it ripped, and then both their mothers rushed out into the garden and caught them.

Henry's mother said it did not matter a bit.

Charlie's mother said it mattered very much indeed and she marched Charlie home straight away, instead of letting him stay for tea-and-*The-Simpsons* as she had previously agreed he could do.

"This is the sort of thing," called Charlie over his shoulder to Henry as he was led away, "that happens to me *all the time!*"

## Going

That was on Wednesday. On Thursday morning Charlie's sad hard life got suddenly sadder and harder. Max was out in the park with a football, his ancient dad was messing about at work with his friends, his ancient mother was messing about at home with the cat, but Charlie was jailed in his bedroom.

7

The day had hardly begun. Charlie had padded downstairs to the empty kitchen, loaded the toaster and been sent back to his room again. Before his toast had even popped up. Simply because, while waiting for his toast, he had prized the free CD off the front of the cereal packet and tried it out in the new computer that his father had just brought home from work.

The computer made grating sounds and

flashed a hundred exciting screens and Charlie's mother came in and yelled, "Back upstairs you go before I completely lose my temper!"

As if she had not completely lost it already.

"What about my toast?" asked Charlie.

"Bother your toast!" shouted Charlie's mother, who grabbed it out of the toaster, flung it into the bin and started trying to get the cereal box disc out of the computer.

"Use a spoon," advised Charlie.

"WHAT?"

"I used a spoon to get it in."

"Charlie," said Charlie's mother in an awful voice. "Vanish!"

At first (except for

missing his toast) Charlie did not mind too much. His PlayStation was in his bedroom, and so was Max's new racing-car game. But it was not long before his mother heard the roaring of car engines and the screech of brakes and stamped upstairs and switched it all off. She seemed to think that Charlie should not be having fun.

For a little while Charlie thought he would leave it all unplugged for ever and that would show how sad and hard his life was.

Then he thought he would plug it all back in again, and that would show his mum.

And then he remembered the conversation in Henry's garden the day before, and he thought he would run away, and that would show everyone.

This seemed the best idea of all, and so he began to pack.

In Max's rucksack he packed his bear, his money box, his photograph album of pictures of himself, and a large bag of stones that he had collected on the beach in case they were valuable. Also he took a trick fly-in-an-ice-cube, a squirting calculator, some plastic dog poo, a half-used packet of itching powder, his last two remaining foaming blood sugar lumps, two socks and one glow-in-the-dark skeleton T-shirt. As a souvenir of his ancient father he took his torch, and as a souvenir of Max he took his stick of seaside rock, but he did not bother taking a souvenir of his mother because she did not own any good stuff.

When he had filled the rucksack he
crept on to the landing and collected two
big holdalls from the little cupboard there.
In one of them he put his PlayStation, and

in the other he put the portable TV that
went with it. In the past Charlie had
moaned about this TV, since it was, as Max
once remarked, the smallest and cheapest

that money could buy. Now he was
thankful that it was not any bigger. Even
as it was, with the rucksack on his back,
the PlayStation holdall across one
shoulder, and the TV across the other, he
could hardly stand up.

Still, he managed, and after a bit of
practice walking up and down his bedroom
it got easier. Everything was fastened to
him, so he could not actually drop
anything, as long as he stayed upright.

Then Charlie, holding tight to the banister,
went very slowly down the
stairs, very slowly through
the kitchen, and
very slowly out of
the door.

Outside the
door he stood on

the path and thought. It seemed all wrong that he was running away without anyone noticing. So very slowly he went back into the house again.

"I'm running away!" he shouted, and then he slammed the door so hard that the last sound he heard from his home was the crack of breaking glass.

Charlie did not look back. He stumped up the garden path and turned on to the street. There he found that a sunny

morning in the school holidays was the worst time possible to run away. There were people everywhere. The first two he met were Lulu, the girl next door, and her best friend Mellie. They were whizzing about on Rollerblades.

"Get out of the way *quick*, Charlie!" they shouted, rushing towards him at a hundred miles an hour.

Charlie could not do anything quick, but his bags saved him from being knocked flat. The heaviness of them rooted him to the ground like a tree stump and the girls bounced off, rubbing their elbows and exclaiming at the hardness of Charlie's corners.

"Where are you going?" they asked. "Aren't you hot, carrying all that? You need a wheelbarrow! You need a lorry!

You've gone all red! What *are* you doing?"

"I'm running away," said Charlie.

"Running!" they repeated.

"Yes, running," said Charlie solidly, and he put his head down and continued his tortoise-like progress for about another ten seconds when he collided with Henry's mother.

"Ouch!" she said. "Charlie! Where *are* you going with all those bags?"

"I'm run—" began Charlie, and then caught sight of the girls, listening and clutching each other and giggling. "I'm walking . . . I'm just walking . . . you know. . ."

"Yes?" asked Henry's mother.

"I'm just walking away," said Charlie and he walked away to show her what he meant and with every step he felt her staring eyes on his breaking back.

It is totally-end-of-the-world Not Fair! grumbled Charlie to himself. I can't even run away in peace!

"Morning, Max!" said the postman, right in front of him.

"I'm not Max," growled Charlie crossly, and he thought, What unbelievable bad luck! The postman now!

"You're not Max?"

"No," said Charlie, swaying under his bags.

"Well, let's get this right," said the postman, as if Charlie had all the time in the world to chat. "There's that Henry, number sixty? Right?"

"I s'pose," groaned Charlie, shrugging his aching shoulders.

"That big dog at number sixty-two, which I don't stop at because he'll have the door down one of these days."

Charlie sighed.

"Madam on wheels over there at number sixty-four?"

Charlie's bags seemed to grow heavier every moment. He shuffled and swayed and longed for the postman to shut up. When he could bear the strain no longer he went and leaned on number sixty-two's fence. The fence leaned too, further and further backwards under his weight. Inside the house a dog went mad.

". . . and so I thought you must be Max," continued the postman, taking no notice of any of this. "Max who gets postcards from America at number sixty-six. . ."

Charlie and the fence were now in a perilous position, halfway between upright and flat on the ground.

"Unless," continued the postman, "you *also* live at number sixty-six *but* you don't get post. Could that be you?"

Charlie nodded, which was a big mistake. The fence collapsed and Charlie buckled at the knees and went down with it. Inside the house the dog ripped down a curtain. Then the front door flew open, the dog charged out and the postman and the lady at number sixty-two started shouting at each other.

Charlie crawled hurriedly away, dragged himself upright at the nearby lamp post and looked around. He felt he needed somewhere to hide, and the only place he could think of was back at his own house, the secret wild patch between the shed and the hedge where he had hidden from trouble all his life.

Two minutes later that was where he was. It felt wonderful. It felt like the far side of the world. It felt like, if you had to run away, then this was the perfect place to go.

*This* is where I am going to stay, thought Charlie happily.

# THREE

## Gone

For a long time Charlie did nothing but lie on his back and suck Max's stick of rock and listen to the faraway sounds of cars and doors and Lulu and Mellie falling over. And then he heard someone come into the garden and knock on the back door. It was Henry's knock, Charlie knew it at once, so when the door opened he listened very hard indeed.

"Did you know your door glass was cracked?" he heard Henry ask.

"Yes, thank you, Henry," said Charlie's mother, perfectly calmly. "Charlie did it."

"Oh," said Henry. "Is he grounded then? Or is he playing?"

"I am sorry, Henry," said Charlie's mother, "but he isn't grounded or playing. He has run away."

"He said he might," said Henry, sounding not a bit surprised. "Where's he gone to, then?"

"Goodness knows," said Charlie's mother. "To sea, perhaps. Or to look for treasure. Somewhere like that, I suppose. I am afraid

I shall have to go now, Henry. I am trying to fix the computer that he wrecked this morning with a disc from a cereal packet which I told him not to put in. It is making a terrible grinding sound and all the text is in Japanese and it is not even our computer. Charlie's father borrowed it from work. . ."

Her voice trailed away. Charlie heard the door close and then a little scratchy noise that he knew was Henry's interested fingers exploring the crack in the glass. Very carefully he stuck his head out into the open and hissed, "Henry!"

Henry gave a great terrified jump.

"I'm here! Behind you!"

"Oh!" exclaimed Henry. "Oh! It's you! I thought you'd run away!"

"I have. To here behind the shed. Come and look!"

"I've seen behind your shed millions of times," grumbled Henry, but he crawled round after Charlie anyway, and looked again.

"It's just the same," he said. "Not very nice."

"I think it's brilliant. No one will ever know I'm here."

"They will if they look behind the shed," said Henry.

"Yes, but they *won't* look behind the shed," replied Charlie. "Dad's too big. Mum's scared of spiders. And Max thinks he's much too important. I'm going to make it all comfy and stay here until they're sorry."

"I think your mum's sorry already," said Henry. "She's sorry you wrecked that computer, anyway."

"That's not the sort of sorry I meant," said Charlie. "Now, go and ask my mum if you can play in our garden."

"Why?"

"Because," said Charlie, "then you will be useful."

Charlie's mother seemed rather surprised to see Henry at the door again. However, she said he could play in the garden if he wanted to, and she hoped he would not be bored.

"I am used to being bored," said Henry. "My family are very boring people."

"Well, just as you please," said Charlie's mother. "I will be in the front room cleaning lemonade-bottle rocket fuel off the carpet. And walls. Do you know how to make a lemonade-bottle rocket, Henry?"

"Oh yes," said Henry. "You partly fill it

with water and pump it up with a bike pump. We did it at school in science."

"Outside or inside?" asked Charlie's mother.

"Outside."

"Last night Charlie discovered that it works just as well inside," said Charlie's mother. "And you don't need water. Orange juice is just as good."

"Is the computer fixed?"

"No. It has Frozen. Oh, Henry, you

might dump this on the bird table for me, as you go past. It is nearly lunch time."

She led him into the kitchen and handed him a large picnic plate. Henry stared at it in astonishment.

"Do you always feed the birds like this at lunch time?" he asked.

"I do since Charlie ran away," said Charlie's mother, and shooed him back into the garden.

Since Charlie had finished Max's stick of rock, starving to death had been one of his biggest worries.

"What is it?" he asked, popping out as soon as his mother had gone.

"Cheese sandwiches, apple

pies, crisps and tomatoes," said Henry, heading for the bird table. "Don't dump it on there! Bring it here! I'm starving."

"You can't eat bird food. You'll drop down dead!"

Charlie did not agree, and after a few minutes of watching him gobble, Henry decided he might be right, and joined in before everything disappeared.

Between bites, Charlie gave orders.

"Carpet," he said. "I shall need a carpet. And a bed. And something to put my drink of water on in the night. And somewhere for my TV and PlayStation and an axe or a very sharp knife. I need to cut a hole in the shed."

"Why do you need to cut a hole in the shed?" demanded Henry.

"You'll see," said Charlie. "Carpet first! What about that Thomas the Tank Engine rug in your bedroom? You're much too old for Thomas! I've thought so for ages."

"You've wanted it for ages, you mean," said Henry, scooping up the last of the crisps. "But I'll fetch it if you like. I'll go now and eat my apple pie on the way. And that sandwich if you don't want it. . ."

Charlie passed it over, and Henry set off. He was back very soon with the rug rolled up under one arm. With his other hand he dragged along his beanbag. This was a horrible thing shaped like a legless purple horse. It had been passed on to

Henry by his cousin Lily, and he had been trying to get rid of it for months.

"It'll do for a bed if you curl up," he said proudly. "And I brought you a tin-opener because I couldn't find an axe or a very sharp knife. Here you are. Now don't wake me up for a bit!"

He curled up on the beanbag, tucked himself up with the Thomas rug and did some pretend snoring.

Charlie, who had already started hacking at the base of the shed with the tin-opener, paused to look at him.

"I'll need my quilt," he said. "And my pillow and my bedside light. I wonder what Mum's doing."

"I'll go and spy on her when I wake up," offered Henry. "I'm very good at spying."

"OK," said Charlie, still busy with the tin-opener.

Henry snored a few more snores and then said, "Charlie, do you think it might get quite boring, living behind this shed?"

"No," said Charlie.

"I'm bored *now*!"

Charlie grunted.

"I think I'll go and start spying."

"Go on then."

Henry crawled out from behind the shed again, across the garden, and crept silently up to the kitchen window.

"Hello, Henry!" said Charlie's mother, popping open the door so unexpectedly that Henry fell over. "Did you get lonely? Come in, if you like. I'm on the phone. To a computer helpline. In a queue. What can I do for you?"

"I was just wondering. . ."

"Mmmm?"

"Now that Charlie's run away. . ."

"Yes, yes? Hurry up! I am moving up the queue."

". . . if you would mind me using his stuff?"

"Using it?"

"Taking it."

"Goodness, no!" said Charlie's mother cheerfully. "Help yourself! We shan't be needing it again, I don't suppose. . . Hello, hello? Oh wonderful! A human voice at last!"

She waved Henry away and hurried into the front room with the phone. Henry, feeling deliciously like a burglar, rushed upstairs to Charlie's bedroom.

"Help yourself!" Charlie's mother had said. Henry did. He found Charlie's quilt, pillow, slippers and pyjamas and flung them out of the window to land on the lawn below. Next he unplugged the bedside lamp and lowered it down by the flex on to the quilt. Finally, he staggered down the stairs with Charlie's bedside table.

It took him less than five minutes. Charlie's mother did not see a thing.

"Brilliant!" said Charlie, when all

these things appeared behind the shed. "Didn't she mind?"

"She said I could," said Henry. "She said she wouldn't be needing it again. She's still trying to get that computer fixed. Crikey! Did you make that great big hole just with a tin-opener?"

"It's good, isn't it?" asked Charlie, and he looked proudly at the results of his work, a jagged hole, easily big enough to get a hand through.

"What's it for?"

"There's plugs in that shed, Henry," said Charlie mysteriously.

"Sink plugs?"

"Electric plugs," said Charlie, "and I can reach them."

By the end of the afternoon Henry's

burglaring and Charlie's hole had changed everything. Now the carpet was down and the bed was made. The bedside lamp was glowing and the PlayStation and TV were unpacked and set up. Charlie and Henry (eating hot pizza, chips and salad absent

mindedly made by Charlie's mother and dumped on the lawn for the cat) were squabbling over the controls.

"I should have run away ages ago," said Charlie.

Henry shared the last chip fairly in half and asked, "What'll you do when I've gone?"

"Gone? Gone where?'

"Home," said Henry.

"Are you going home?"

"*I* haven't run away," Henry reminded him.

Charlie suddenly didn't want his last half chip. All at once, life behind the shed seemed much less cosy. Still he said bravely, "I expect I'll stay up all night. I've always wanted to. When are you going, so I can get started?"

"Now," said Henry.

"*Now?*"

"Yes," said Henry, and went.

## Gone for hours

After Henry had gone there followed a time when Charlie became so bored his stomach ached and he thought he must be ill.

Suddenly there were footsteps in the garden: Max, pushing his bike round the corner of the house.

"Hi, Max!" he heard his mother call.

37

"Did you have a good time?"

"Yes, thanks," said Max.

"Supper very soon, when Dad comes home. Just the three of us, because Charlie's run away."

"He has?" asked Max. "Oh superb! Fantastic! At last!"

Behind the shed Charlie pulled awful faces at Max. He was still pulling them when his father came home.

This time both Max and his mother rushed out to tell the news.

"Charlie's run away!" they said happily. "It's been so peaceful. We can't imagine where he's gone but he's definitely completely vanished!"

Charlie's father had already heard what had happened to the computer, and had just been stopped by the owner of number sixty-two and shown the remains of the fence. So he was not in a good mood. He said it should not be hard to find Charlie.

"Just a matter of following the trail of destruction he leaves everywhere he goes!" he said.

"No, no," said Charlie's mother. "You do not understand! He's been gone for hours; he must be miles away by now. Poor Henry has had to play on his own here all afternoon."

"Henry's not run away too, then?" asked Charlie's father in a hopeful kind of voice.

"Oh no," said Charlie's mother. "Henry

would not have to do that. Charlie told me this morning that Henry is far better looked after than he is. He does not have a horrible rotten mother always fussing. Or a bossy big brother or a father who never shares his stuff. I am terribly sorry about the computer. I had only turned my back for a minute to get the parachute off the cat. . . Charlie made her a parachute, you see, very early this morning, before he got up. Poor old Suzy!"

I was being kind! thought Charlie, listening indignantly. I was *helping* her! She was sitting very dangerously on the banister without a parachute!

"So that's what happened to my football shirt!" grumbled Max. "I wondered why it was all tied up with bits of string."

It was an emergency! thought Charlie. Which is most important, your football shirt or our faithful only cat?

"Poor old Max," Charlie heard his father say as they all went inside.

Poor old Max now! thought Charlie, all alone again. What about poor old Charlie! Having to live out here behind the shed! All by myself! In the dark! In the. . .

Something cold hit Charlie on the face.

"RAIN!" exclaimed Charlie.

It was true it was raining. Slow, heavy drops were falling on Charlie, and

Charlie's bed and bedside lamp, and worst
of all, on Charlie's portable TV and
PlayStation.

"Oh!" thought Charlie, frantically
unplugging and stuffing and packing.
"What shall I do?"

He had two choices, he realized. He
could either go home and put up with his
awful family, or he would go somewhere
further away. Somewhere dry and comfy.

By the time he had his bags packed his mind was made up. He pushed the Thomas rug and beanbag into the shed, picked up his backpack and his impossibly heavy bags, draped his quilt over his shoulders like a cloak and headed off down the road to Henry's house.

Luckily, Henry's back door was open and there was no one in the kitchen. From the living room came the sound of the TV and of Henry's mother talking on the phone. Charlie crept up the stairs and past the bathroom. Henry's bedroom was empty too, but from the bathroom came terrific splashing and Henry's voice ordering, "Dive, dive, dive!" Silently Charlie lowered his bags to the floor, and flopped down on Henry's bed.

Henry was very surprised to find that Charlie had run away to his house, but he was not sorry. He had felt rather left out, coming home alone and leaving all the adventures to Charlie.

So he willingly helped Charlie hide his belongings in the cupboard, fetched him the biscuit tin and went downstairs to ask for two mugs of hot chocolate instead of one.

"Two?" asked his mother, and she said into the telephone, "Henry has just come in and asked if he can have two hot chocolates! He must be extra thirsty. . ."

Henry put on his extra thirsty face.

"Of course you can," she said to Henry.

"And two baths if you like, and two pairs of pyjamas. . ."

Whoever she was talking to laughed. Henry heard them.

". . . but then bed, and no talking. . ."

"Talking?" asked Henry, startled.

". . . to that hamster. . . Shall I come and tuck you up?"

"I will tuck myself up, thank you," said Henry angelically, "to save you bothering."

Charlie stayed hidden at Henry's house for thirty-nine hours. He knew it was that long, because he counted.

It was a time of great quietness.

Food was the easy part. Henry was always appearing with piles of the stuff. Henry's mother seemed to leave it lying around in uncounted heaps: bunches of

bananas,
sausage rolls,
cartons of fruit juice,
boxes of cereal, cheese
sticks and sandwiches.

"I should like
toast," said Charlie.

Henry brought toast
but it was not like home toast. It
was made with the wrong sort of bread and
spread with the wrong sort of butter. It did
not smell right, either.

"You're too fussy," said Henry crossly,
when Charlie complained. "You'd better
eat as much as you can, whether you like it
or not. I might not be able to get any more
for ages."

Henry said this with everything he
brought. He made it sound like starvation

46

might happen any moment. Charlie ate until he was stuffed and ungrateful. When Henry appeared on Friday afternoon with a plateful of warm-out-of-the-oven chocolate cakes, Charlie pushed them out of sight under the bed. All that night he could smell them there, and it made him feel awful.

The nights were very long. Charlie slept on Henry's floor, with Henry's sleeping bag underneath him, and his own quilt on top. It was not like a sleepover because they could not talk. It was as uninteresting as going to bed at home, except that instead of Max telling ghost stories for company, he had Henry snoring and muttering and tossing the bedclothes about.

But the days were worse than the nights.

During the day Henry and Charlie
played silently with every game that Henry
owned. They made models out of every
piece of Lego. They fitted together every
jigsaw puzzle.

It was terribly boring for Charlie, but it
was all right for Henry. When he grew
tired of the silent bedroom life he could
escape. He could tear round the garden
kicking goals into his football net. He
could watch TV in
the living room,
or scrape out a
cake bowl in the
kitchen.

Best of all, he
could be noisy. He
could jump down
the stairs with

enormous crashes. He could ring his bike bell or chatter to the man mending the fence at number sixty-two, or yell across the garden to Lulu. Charlie, listening to these happy sounds, felt more and more like a prisoner.

"Not a prisoner!" said Henry, insulted, when Charlie told him this. "More like a . . . like a . . . like a pet! Like Hammy!"

Hammy was Henry's hamster. He also lived in Henry's bedroom, constantly supplied with delicious food and terrible toys. He also kept his extra supplies under the bed.

Sometimes Hammy bit people.

Charlie could understand why.

## No Charlie

Charlie could never have survived the thirty-nine hours in Henry's bedroom if it wasn't for one thing.

His family.

After Charlie ran away, Charlie's family took to visiting Henry's family very often. They seemed to need to talk about Charlie. They would sit in the garden under

Henry's bedroom window and talk and talk. Charlie could hear every word.

At first their visits were quite cheerful. They talked in loud cheerful voices about what a good time they were having without Charlie, and what an even better time he must be having without them.

But by Friday afternoon, when Charlie had been gone for a whole day and a night, things were changing.

Charlie's dad started it. He began to complain. He complained about the quietness at home.

"Quiet makes me jumpy," he said. "Max is never any good at being properly noisy. Not, you know, *totally* noisy. I don't know why, but he can never seem to manage it. . . We miss Charlie, for noise."

This pleased Charlie very much, and he

could understand it too. Quietness had never been his favourite thing, and lately it had begun to drive him mad.

The next person to complain was Max. Max said he was bored, and this must have been true because it took hardly any persuading to get him to be a goalie for Henry.

Max stopped twenty goals in a row, the last five with his hands behind his back to prove how useless Henry was at football.

Henry said no wonder Charlie had run away.

"What do you know about Charlie running away?" asked Max.

"I know a lot," said Henry, looking at Max with sinister half-closed eyes to pay him back for stopping all his goals.

"Do you think he'll ever come back?"

"Nope!"

"I bet he's getting pretty hungry by now."

"I bet he isn't," said Henry.

"Cold too, at night."

"Boiling hot," said Henry firmly.

"It's not much fun at home without him. Mum and Dad have no one to moan at except me."

"You'll get used to it," said Henry. "It's my turn in goal. Come on."

So Max shot twenty goals past Henry, the last three with his eyes shut, and

Henry said he wasn't playing any more.

"Were you watching?" he asked Charlie in bed that night. "Did you see how hard your rotten brother kicked that ball?"

"Much less hard than usual," said Charlie. "He was hardly trying."

"What's he like when he tries, then?"

"Fantastic. Do you think he's missing me?"

"No."

"Not even a bit?"

"No."

"I think," said Charlie, "he's missing me a lot."

"Henry and Hammy!" called Henry's mother up the stairs. "Shush now!"

So they shushed, and Charlie soon fell asleep, tired out with doing nothing. He woke on Saturday morning to the sound of Max's voice, calling up under the bedroom window.

"Henry!"

"What?" asked Henry. "What? What is it? Oh, Max! What d'you want?"

"Tell Charlie there's a great big parcel just come for him at our house!"

"All right," said Henry. "I'll tell him. . ."

"Ha!" said Max, sounding extremely pleased.

". . . if I ever see him again!"

Max stamped home, defeated, and later

Charlie sent Henry to collect his parcel.

"How?" asked Henry.

"Just ask," Charlie said. "They'll let you have it. They let you have my other stuff, didn't they?"

Charlie was right. They did let Henry have it. He returned to Charlie in triumph and Charlie tore off the wrappers and found a double-barrelled supersonic water-squirter, the perfect present from his Uncle Pete, exactly what he had been wanting all summer.

"I need to try it out!" he said.

"Where?"

Charlie looked around. It was true

that upstairs in someone else's bedroom was not the place to test a double-barrelled water-squirter.

"Out the window," he said at last.

"You can't," said Henry. "Your mum's out there. Grumbling to my mum. About toast."

"Toast?" asked Charlie, suddenly interested. "Toast!" And he crept to the window to listen.

". . . so much in the habit," he heard. "I've got so much in the habit of making stacks of toast for Charlie that I can't seem to stop! I've done it again this morning! The bird table's piled high. The cat won't touch it. I just can't get used to him being gone. . ."

She sounded so sad that Charlie could hardly bear it.

"I should write myself a reminder and

stick it on the toaster..."

Charlie's eyes prickled with tears.

"... saying NO CHARLIE..."

Charlie could endure it no more. It wasn't having a water-squirter and nowhere to squirt it. It wasn't because Max was missing him so much he had to play football with Henry. It wasn't the quietness that made his father jumpy.

It was the thought of that label on the toaster.

He pushed past Henry and ran down the stairs, through the door, past his amazed mother, out of the garden and along the street and into his own familiar kitchen. And by the time Henry caught up with him, it was like a party in there. A toast party, with a water fight afterwards, Charlie and Henry against Max and Lulu and Mellie, with the dads joining in, and the mothers hugging each other, and everyone saying, "Oh, isn't it wonderful! Charlie's come home!"

"I never ran away myself," remarked Max, when he and Charlie were finally in bed that night. "What's it like?"

"Fantastic," said Charlie.

"What's the best bit?"

"Oh," said Charlie. "The last bit, I

think. Coming home. And everyone being
sorry. And then forgiving them all. Like a
hero. . ."

Max smiled in the dark.

". . . like me!" said Charlie.